CROW CALL

LOIS LOWRY

Illustrated by
BAGRAM IBATOULLINE

SCHOLASTIC PRESS / NEW YORK

Library of Congress Cataloging-in-Publication Data is available.
ISBN-13: 978-0-545-03035-9
ISBN-10: 0-545-03035-8

10 9 8 7 6 5 4 3 2 1   09 10 11 12 13

Printed in Singapore   46
First edition, October 2009

The display type was set in P22 Terra Cotta.
The text was set in Times Roman.
The art was created using watercolor and acryl-gouache on paper.
Book design by Elizabeth B. Parisi

FOR MY BROTHER, JON
AND IN MEMORY OF MY SISTER, HELEN
— L. L.

IN MEMORY OF ANDREW WYETH,
MY FAVORITE
AMERICAN ARTIST
— B. I.

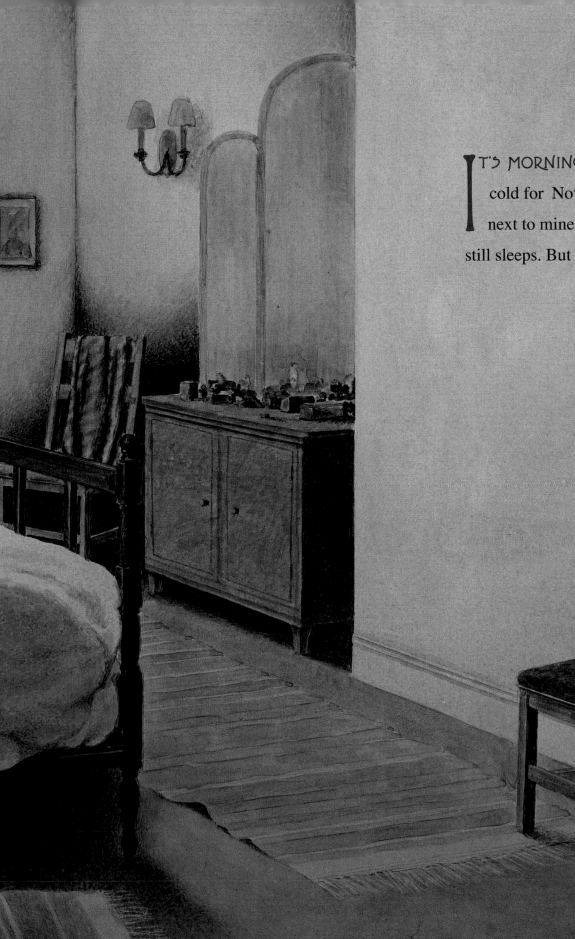

IT'S MORNING, EARLY, BARELY LIGHT, cold for November. At home, in the bed next to mine, Jessica, my older sister, still sleeps. But my bed is empty.

I sit shyly in the front seat of the car next to the stranger who is my father,

my legs pulled up under the too-large wool shirt I am wearing.

   I practice his name to myself, whispering it under my breath. *Daddy. Daddy.*

Saying it feels new. The war has lasted so long. He has been gone so long.

Finally I look over at him timidly and speak aloud.

"Daddy," I say, "I've never gone hunting before. What if I don't know what to do?"

"Well, Liz," he says, "I've been thinking about that, and I've decided to put you in charge of the crow call. Have you ever operated a crow call?"

I shake my head. "No."

"It's an art," he says. "No doubt about that. But I'm pretty sure you can handle it. Some people will blow and blow on a crow call and not a single crow will even wake up or bother to listen, much less answer. But I really think you can do it. Of course," he adds, chuckling, "having that shirt will help."

My father had bought the shirt for me. In town to buy groceries, he had noticed my hesitating in front of Kronenberg's window. The plaid hunting shirts had been in the store window for a month—the popular red-and-black and green-and-black ones toward the front, clothing mannequins holding duck decoys; but my shirt, the rainbow plaid, hung separately on a wooden hanger toward the back of the display. I had lingered in front of Kronenberg's window every chance I had since the hunting shirts had appeared.

My sister had rolled her eyes in disdain. "Daddy," she pointed out to him as we entered Kronenberg's, "that's a *man's* shirt."

The salesman had smiled and said dubiously, "I don't quite think . . . "

"You know, Lizzie," my father had said to me as the salesman wrapped the shirt, "buying this shirt is probably a very practical thing to do. You will never *ever* outgrow this shirt."

Now, as we go into a diner for breakfast, the shirt unfolds itself downward until the bottom of it reaches my knees; from the bulky thickness of rolled-back cuffs, my hands are exposed. I feel totally surrounded by shirt.

My father orders coffee for himself. The waitress asks, "What about your boy? What does he want?"

My father winks at me, and I hope that my pigtails will stay hidden inside the plaid wool collar. Holding my head very still, I look at the menu. At home my usual breakfast is cereal with honey and milk. My mother keeps honey in a covered silver pitcher. There's no honey on the diner's menu.

"What's your favorite thing to eat in the whole world?" asks my father.

I smile at him. "Cherry pie," I admit. If he hadn't been away for so long, he would have known. My mother had even put birthday candles on a cherry pie on my last birthday. It was a family joke in a family that hadn't included Daddy.

My father hands back both menus to the waitress. "Three pieces of cherry pie," he tells her.

"Three?" She looks at him sleepily, not writing the order down. "You mean two?"

"No," he said, "I mean three. One for me, with black coffee, and two for my hunting companion, with a large glass of milk."

She shrugs.

We eat quickly, watching the sun rise across the Pennsylvania farmlands. Back in the car, I flip my pigtails out from under my shirt collar and giggle.

"Hey, boy," my father says to me in an imitation of the groggy waitress's voice, "you sure you can eat all that cherry pie, boy?"

"Just you watch me, lady," I answer in a deep voice, pulling my face into stern, serious lines. We laugh again, driving out into the gray-green hills of the early morning.

It's not far to the place he has chosen, not long until he pulls the car to the side of the empty road and stops.

Grass, frozen after its summer softness, crunches under our feet; the air is sharp and supremely clear, free from the floating pollens of summer, and our words seem etched and breakable on the brittle stillness. I feel the smooth wood of the crow call in my pocket, moving my fingers against it for warmth, memorizing its ridges and shape. I stamp my feet hard against the ground now and then as my father does. I want to scamper ahead of him like a puppy, kicking the dead leaves and reaching the unknown places first, but there is an uneasy feeling along the edge of my back at the thought of walking in front of someone who is a *hunter*. The word makes me uneasy. Carefully I stay by his side.

It is quieter than summer. There are no animal sounds, no bird-waking noises; even the occasional leaf that falls within our vision does so in silence, spiraling slowly down to blend in with the others. But most leaves are already gone from the trees; those that remain catch there by accident, waiting for the wind that will free them. Our breath is steam.

"Daddy," I ask shyly, "were you scared in the war?"

He looks ahead, up the hill, and after a moment he says, "Yes. I was scared."

"Of what?"

"Lots of things. Of being alone. Of being hurt. Of hurting someone else."

"Are you still?"

He glances down. "I don't think so. Those kinds of scares go away."

"I'm scared sometimes," I confide.

He nods, unsurprised. "I know," he said. "Are you scared now?"

I start to say no. Then I remember the word that scares me. *Hunter*.

I answer, "Maybe a little."

I look at his gun, his polished, waxed prize, and then at him. He nods, not saying anything. We walk on.

"Daddy?"

"Mmmmmm?" He is watching the sky, the trees.

"I wish the crows didn't eat the crops."

"They don't know any better," he says. "Even people do bad things without meaning to."

"Yes, but . . ." I pause and then say what I'd been thinking. "They might have babies to take care of. Baby crows."

"Not now, Liz, not this time of year," he says. "By now their babies are grown. It's a strange thing, but by now they don't even know who their babies are." He puts his free arm over my shoulders for a moment.

"And their babies grow up and eat the crops, too," I say, and sigh, knowing it to be true and unchangeable.

"It's too bad," he says. We begin to climb the hill.

"Can you call anything else, Daddy? Or just crows?"

"Sure," he says. "Listen. *Mooooooooo*. That's a cow call."

"Guess the cows didn't hear it," I tease.

"Well, of course, sometimes they choose not to answer. I can do tigers, too. *Rrrrrrrrrr*."

"Ha. So can I. And bears. Better watch out, now. Bears might come out of the woods on this one. *Grrrrrrrrrr*."

"You think you're so smart, doing bears. Listen to this. Giraffe call." He stands with his neck stretched out, soundless.

I try not to laugh, wanting to do rabbits next, but I can't keep from it. He looks so funny, with his neck pulled away from his shirt collar and a condescending, poised, giraffe look on his face. I giggle at him and we keep walking to the top of the hill.

From where we stand, we can see almost back to town. We can look down on our car and follow the ribbon of road through the farmlands until it is lost in trees. Dark roofs of houses lay scattered, separated by pastures.

"Okay, Lizzie," says my father, "this is a good place. You can do the crow call now."

I see no crows. For a moment, the fear of disappointing him struggles with my desire to blow into the smooth, polished tip of the crow call. But I see that he's waiting, and I take it from my pocket, hold it against my lips, and blow softly.

The harsh, muted sound of a sleepy crow comes as a surprise to me, and I smile at it, at the delight of having made that sound myself. I do it again, softly.

From a grove of trees on another hill comes an answer from a waking bird. Just one, and then silence.

Tentatively I call again, more loudly. The branches of a nearby tree rustle, and crows answer, fluttering and calling crossly. They fly briefly into the air and then settle on a branch—three of them.

"Look, Daddy," I whisper. "Do you see them? They think *I'm* a crow!"

He nods, watching them.

I move away from him and stand on a rock at the top of the hill and blow loudly several times. Crows rise from all the trees. They scream with harsh voices and I respond, blowing again and again as they fly from the hillside in circles, dipping and soaring, landing speculatively, lurching from the limbs in afterthought and then settling again with resolute and disgruntled shrieks.

"Listen, Daddy! Do you hear them? They think I'm their friend! Maybe their baby, all grown up!"

I run about the top of the hill and then down, through the frozen grass, blowing the crow call over and over. The crows call back at me, and from all the trees they rise, from all the hills. They circle and circle, and the morning is filled with the patterns of calling crows as I look back, still running. I can see my father sitting on a rock, and I can see he is smiling.

My crow calling comes in shorter and shorter spurts as I become breathless; finally I stop and stand laughing at the foot of the hill, and the noise from the crows subsides as they circle and settle back in the trees. They are waiting for me.

My father comes down the hill to meet me coming up. He carries his gun carefully; and though I am grateful to him for not using it, I feel that there is no need to say thank you—Daddy knows this already. The crows will always be there and they will always eat the crops; and some other morning, on some other hill, a hunter, maybe not my daddy, will take aim.

I blow the crow call once more, to say good morning and good-bye and everything that goes in between. Then I put it into the pocket of my shirt and reach over, out of my enormous cuff, and take my father's hand.

Lois Lowry as a child, wearing the plaid shirt featured in this book. Of *Crow Call*,
she says, "The details of this story are true. They happened in 1945, to me and
my father. But parents and children groping toward understanding each other — that
happens to everyone. And so this story is not really just *my* story, but everyone's."